Clint Faraday
book 32
Blood and Gold

Clint receives a call from Sergio Sanchez, head of violent crimes for Isla Colón and the Bocas archipelago. An elderly woman living near The Bluffs was found with her dead when the maid came to work. Her throat was cut. She was in front of a large safe that was unopened.

Clint goes to investigate. He quickly locates the combination to the old safe and opens it to find stacks of gold bars.

Sergio had said it was a lot of blood. Clint said there was also a lot of gold!

The woman always lived frugally. Where did the money come from? Who knew about it and killed her?

Contents

About the author

CD Moulton has traveled extensively over much of the world both in the music business, where he was a rock guitarist, songwriter and arranger and in an import/export business. He has been everything from a bar owner to auto salvage (junkyard) manager, longshoreman to high steel worker, orchid grower to landscaper, tropical fish farmer to commercial fisherman. He started writing books in 1983 and has published more than 350 books as of January 1, 2023. His most popular books to date are about research with orchids, though much of his science fiction and fantasy work has proven popular. He wrote the CD Grimes, PI series, and the Det. Nick Storie series, Clint Faraday series, and many other works.

He now resides in Gualaca, Chiriqui, Panamá, where he writes books, plays music with friends, does research with orchids and medicinal plants. He has lately become involved in fighting for the rights of the indigenous people, who are among his closest friends, and in fighting the extreme corruption in the courts and police in Panamá.

He offers the free e-book, *Fading Paradise*, that explains what he has been through because of the corruption.

CD is the discoverer of the Chadam Protocol for curing cancer.

Facebook page Ambrosia peruviana for cancer.

Blood and Gold

Golden Sunrise

Clint Faraday, retired PI from Florida, shifted his eight month old son a bit and took another drink of coffee. He was laying on his hammock on the deck of his house on Saigon Bay, Bocas Town, Isla Colón, Bocas del Toro, Panamá, to watch the play of golden colors of the sunrise over the Caribbean. There were a lot of clouds close to the horizon to make sunrises spectacular.

After the sun was up a bit and his cup was empty, he went for his morning swim. The water was a very comfortable temperature. Little Nito (Clintonito Faraday) could already stay afloat on his own. Clint had done as his Indio friends and family in raising his son in the traditions of the comarca. If you lived on the water, your children should learn to respect it and enjoy it, not fear it. If introduced to being in water at a very young age, the rest would come naturally.

Tyna, his beautful Ngobe wife, came out on the deck to bring his breakfast. She took Nito onto the deck while Clint swam strongly for about fifteen minutes, to Judi Lum's dock. She was his attractive next door neighbor, who often helped him with his cases. She had an uncanny knack for finding information.

Clint climbed onto the deck, rinsed, and slipped on a bathing suit. He never dressed until he decided what he was going to do each morning. Today would be fixing up things around the place. He had just come back to the island two days ago. He was raising his child mainly on the comarca.

After his breakfast of fresh papaya, melon, cantaloupe and pineapple, he went inside and checked his e-mail and such, erased the twenty some-odd spam/scam messages, answered his brother's e-mail birthday greeting (he was sixty one just two days ago), wrote replies to several others, then went out to start checking for the little things that went wrong when a house wasn't used for four months. His friends and neighbors took good care of the place for him when he was away.

At a few minutes after eight his phone buzzed. It was Sergio Valdez, head of violent crimes for the Bocas del Toro archipelago, so he answered.

"Clint? Sergio Sanchez here. Are you busy this morning?"

"Like usual, Sergio. How are things?"

"As usual, with the exception of a body. I know you just got back, but thought you might be interested."

"It's something to do. Details?"

"Madeline West, the elderly woman out here just past the bluffs, was found by the maid when she came to work. Her throat's been cut. She was tortured a bit, I think. There's a lot of blood."

"Maddy? The woman in that little cottage back under the giant mango tree?"

"Yes. You knew her. Everyone did, though she was a little bit of a recluse. She's been here for more than thirty five years. We still didn't know much about her. I've been in the house a couple of times. I never knew she had a big safe in the bedroom. Doc theorizes that she was tortured for the combination. They didn't get it. The thing's not open and doesn't look like it has been in a lot of years."

"Hmm. She was what we call frugal back in Florida. I thought she only had a small Social Security deposit every month from the states. She was from the Denver area. An ex-pat who was living here because it's the best place to live on a small income. Isla Colón's getting too expensive for that, now.

"You're there? I'll get my bike and come out. I want to run it some. Ben and Earl ride once in awhile, but it doesn't do it any good to just sit here. Maybe I'll spot something."

They chatted a few minutes while Clint dressed

and kissed Tyna goodbye and got the Ducatti out from it's lockup on the side of the house. He headed out to The Bluffs and just past. The police truck was parked in the front yard, next to the ambulance. He parked between them and went in. Sergio called that he was in the bedroom. They hadn't moved the body yet.

He went in. Sergio waved to the body. She was lying in front of a large old safe. Sergio went out and Doc came in. He said they didn't have a clue as to how to open the thing. There probably wasn't much in it.

Clint looked over the scene. Messy.

This type of person would have the combination somewhere only she could decode. It wouldn't be too hard to find and it wouldn't be in an obvious place.

He quickly looked through the drawers. Everything was neat and clean. Handkerchiefs and small costume jewelry and such in a top drawer. Underwear in the drawer under it. A cabinet door beneath to the floor level. There were shoes and a sewing basket there.

So it went with all the drawers and cabinets. He thought a moment and decided the combination would be in that room. What was out of place?

Only that sewing basket. That kind of thing was in the little den area with the books.

There was nothing in the sewing basket. Doc had the crew move the body to the ambulance. He soon left.

Clint went back into the den. What was out of place there?

He looked over the hundreds of books on their shelves and noted there was a recipe book among the mysteries. All the recipes he had found to then were in the kitchen. That made that one out of place in an unnoticeable way.

He flipped through the book. Several of the recipes had notations in the margins.

The book had 114 pages. The big dial on the safe had 100 numbers. It was an old four number combination type, most likely.

He went back through the book, looking for anything added that used a number less than one hundred. Most of them.

The notations in the margins didn't fit anything.

He was sure they had something to do with what he was looking for. He didn't see what, then shook his head and went back through. There were four pages with notations that began with numbers. Page thirteen had *2 cups flour* to start the recipe addition. Page eighty four had *1 cup sugar* to start it. Page thirty one had *4 tblspn butter* to start it. Page seven had *3 eggs, beaten* to start it. The rest had no numbers starting them.

Clint caught that immediately. The combination was 84-13-7-31.

He went back into the bedroom and tried the combination. It worked. The door came open just as Sergio came back into the room to remark, "There was a lot of blood in this one!"

Clint was staring into the safe. It had a space of two feet by eighteen inches four feet high. It was stacked solidly with shiny gold bars. There was possibly enough room left inside to hold one, maximum two, more bars. One of them had a stamped legend showing on the side:

Bank of Mexico
15/05/39
60 Oz WS

"There's also a lot of gold." Clint replied. "I'd say probably three thousand bars at sixty world standard ounces. That gives us eighteen thousand ounces. Gold is more than fifteen hundred dollars an ounce, today. Off my head, that's twenty seven or twenty eight million dollars. It was worth a third of that twenty years ago when she put it here. Of course, the dollar would buy three times as much, back then. The number's changed. The value's about the same."

"Ten million, thirty million. Either one's a whole lot of money," Sergio said. "You have to wonder where it came from."

"That's a very important point we'll have to investigate," Clint said. "I think our answers will be mostly back then. We have to be sure this isn't something done by someone who saw the safe and didn't know what was inside. They figured it had to be worth something, she wouldn't open it, that made them think it was a lot more than they first guessed. They tried too hard to ger her to tell them the combination. It's altogether possible she didn't remember it and wouldn't tell them where it was. She knew who they were. She had to die."

"A very possible scenario. It still leaves us with the original question: where did it come from?"

"You get no argument from me. We'll have to see if we can find out. I don't see anything else here, but I'll want to go through the books and her letters or whatever else we can find. She may have left it in a diary ... she wasn't the diary type. Maybe there's something."

"We shall see. I'll leave a man here to watch the place. You can open the safe anytime, so lock it up. Only you and I have seen it. We leave the impression there wasn't anything in it."

Clint nodded and locked the safe.

He wondered how they were going to move it. It was thick steel that weighed several hundred pounds, plus half a ton of gold. Eight people lifting would be max. Each one would have to lift more than two hundred pounds.

Give the problem to the Indios. They would, no doubt, come up with something that was simple and effective. Or simply logical and practical. For the time being, so long as no one knew there was anything in the safe, it didn't really matter. He could think of one simple and practical method: take the gold bars *out* of the safe and move them separately.

One thing was damned certain. No one was going to steal that safe. If they couldn't open it, the gold was as secure there as anywhere.

Clint sat in Sergio's office to discuss what they had to find. That the gold would prove important was foregone, though it may not be behind the murder except for the fact it was there. There was someone local who tried to get the combination from her, she was too stubborn to give it to them or didn't remember it, they had gone too far, she knew them, they killed her.

There were a very mixed bag of people here. The Bluffs were a distance from Bocas Town, off the road to Boca del Drago. There were gringos, blacks, Indios, Mestizos, Spanish and mixes with Chinese and whatever else. Some of them had a far less than a good reputation with the police and with their neighbors, though most were regular people. Their were a couple Clint had run across who were known to break into houses to steal things. The laws here made it as much as impossible to prosecute anyone under seventeen. The parents must agree to having them prosecuted. Too many grew up with the thought they were immune to any kind of retaliation for what they did. Those usually ended up in jail at eighteen and spent a good part of the rest of their lives there.

This case didn't have that flavor unless it was someone only a few months from legal age.

There didn't seem to be anything missing from the house. That factor was disturbing and would point to someone from outside. That would point to it being someone from her past, who knew exactly what was in that safe. What was there was safe enough if they didn't have and didn't find the combination. Clint found it because he had experience with the psychological types who would leave it somewhere that most people wouldn't recognize or consider. Maddy wasn't the type to write it on the back of her address book or hide it behind a picture, but she was the type who would write it somewhere. A code only she knew was a good bet. There it was.

Another thing is that the local people wouldn't think she had anything to steal. Even if they knew about the safe, they would think it was there and she used it, if at all, for the titulo and insurance policies or whatever. Clint had seen her at the bank the second Wednesday of the month, several times, so people would figure, as he did, that she got her regular social security deposit the second Wednesday of the month. According to the way she lived, that was all she had. She had a couple of old things in the house that had some value. Currier and Ives dishes, a real crystal punch bowl and cups. That kind of thing is identifiable. They wouldn't know how to get rid of it if they had it.

The more he thought about this, the less he believed it was anyone local, unless it was someone from the states or somewhere who was living here for a while.

He talked with Sergio about his theories. Her past would be checked as carefully as possible, but going back thirty five years or more meant she would be on the computers only minimally. They were looking for something that happened thirty five to forty years ago. Something that involved a half ton of gold bars.

"Sergio, check with Mexico. Find out what happened there, a bank robbery or something. Half a ton of gold marked with the seal of the Bank of Mexico has to have left something to trace. It was worth a hell of a lot, even then. I know it leveled at six hundred for a long period about then. That was just before the rise that's continuing today."

"I thought of that. I'm having it checked. It helps that we have the date it was poured into those bars.

"Clint, we have to go out there and check those bars! If they're all the same date, we have a very likely scenario! A very traceable scenario!"

Clint nodded. It was a starting point.

"Sergio, maybe that gold wasn't stolen that far back. We'll have to check from nineteen thirty nine until nineteen seventy seven."

It was Sergio's turn to nod. "Yes. It's entirely possible it was stored somewhere for years. A second theft? Someone found it years later and stole it, themselves?"

"So we have to check that thirty eight years. That's a bit longer and harder a search."

Sergio sighed. He and Clint took the truck to Maddy's place. They checked the safe. The bars all seemed to have that same date stamped onto them.

"I'm wishing gold rusted or changed color or something," Sergio complained. "We could then determine how long ago it was cast."

Clint raised an eyebrow and thought. "Yeah. We may have something from somewhere else. What the stamp says is what the stamp says. It could have been stamped with that date a week ago or a hundred years ago."

"No. It would not be stamped with a date later than the actual date. If anyone were to find it, the situation would be obvious. We're left with thirty eight years to check, seriously, and a few more, just in case."

"Also; anything or everything on the stamp could be false. All we can be certain of is ... nothing. I was going to say it was stamped the same day, so was melted and cast in one day. Not so realistic. Some could have been done ten years before the next.

"Sergio, this is getting interesting! I think we have to go over this house and the sheds and grounds completely! I think I saw something!"

Sergio looked at him expectantly.

"That little shed in back. It has a sugar boiler."

"A lot of the ... she never boiled down sugar.

"She might have, Clint. I think she did one time say she made her own syrup."

"I suppose, but it looked used. She could boil down enough syrup for five years in a day. I think I've seen something that opens this up even more, now. It could damned well be a local."

Sergio thought and nodded slowly. "A local who saw the lady melting down some gold and casting it into a bar that she took into the house. The problem I have with that is that there wasn't room in that safe for another bar. The safe wasn't opened recently. You noted that."

"I'm thinking of another avenue to research. The time makes it likely that something happened that would mean this murder wouldn't have happened, say, a year ago."

"We have quite enough avenues to explore now, thank you!"

They started their search. Only Clint and Sergio would handle it. They didn't want to have to explain to any team what they were looking for or why.

Clint went through the little shed where the sugar boiler was kept. He found several smaller boiling pans, but nothing definite. A careful search found a small globule of gold, about the size of a lentil, but no more.

The next shed was where she kept the little fishing tackle, lawnmower, Weedeater, and portable gas stove that had been used recently. It was a definite possibility. It had a kettle-sized burner, which would produce enough heat to melt gold.

Sergio called. He was checking the shed where she had a small pump to fill her water tank from the small stream there. It was small and hardly more than covered the pump and switchboard – and a double mold, exactly the size and shape of the gold bars.

"We have to find the stamp," he said. "These are commercial sixty ounce molds."

Clint nodded. They made a very careful search. There was no stamp anywhere on the property.

"Maybe something was taken from the house,"

Sergio suggested.

"I think there was. It wasn't that stamp. Let's go back to the station and check our victim's past. I think maybe there's going to be a lot to learn about her, personally. We still have to find a connection."

"We have to find a lot of connections, but one would be a start. Which one do you think is top priority, now?"

"Who went to jail in thirty nine or forty and just got out."

"Why would someone be in jail for that long? Other than murder, I don't see it."

"Murder, other than hers, is probably a big part of this. I think we'll be looking for a murderer. I think that was a time when this was even possible. The world was just then getting into a world war. Things without military significance could slip by.

"There's another little thing that could apply here. Huge amounts of gold and silver were being moved to places that the holders felt were safer than bank vaults. A lot of gold and silver was stored in Mexico. If it was marked as to source, that could identify the wrong people, particularly politicians in a number of countries, it would be melted down and identified as bank security holdings.

"Sergio, I have to collect some facts about the

little lady. She was what? Eighty years old? She would have been a young woman, then. She might have been involved with people who had access to gold bars for any number of reasons."

"She was eighty four two months ago. She was born in twenty eight. She would have only been eleven years old in thirty nine."

"Crap!"

"We'll have to check who her parents were and what happened to them. They would have been the right age to pull something off."

They went back to the station. Sergio would get busy with a computer search of Madeline West's past. Clint went home and called to Judi Lum, his neighbor, who was on her deck, working with her plants. He got an idea and said he was coming over. He had something to discuss with her.

"Judi, see what you can learn about Maddy West. There are a couple of the people in the garden club and so forth who knew her for years. See if anyone came here recently who had contact with her or if anyone was asking questions about her."

"She was a regular at the garden club. She was friends with Yveth and Carolina, particularly. They're in their seventies and were the closest to her age. Yveth was born here, Carolina was from Pastore. I think they knew her since she came here.

"I do remember one thing that seemed odd. Yveth was talking about the time when she was having her house built. She told Ramón her name was Marge. When Yveth asked why, she said she did that sometimes, because her uncle used to call her Margie, from the TV show, *My Little Margie*, because she looked like the girl who played the part. When she was thinking of something else, she sometimes said her name was Margie."

"So. We have to look for a name change from Margie to Maddy."

"Yes. If a person changes her name, there's usually a pretty good reason for it. What else might she have changed?"

Clint agreed and went to play with Nito and tease Tyna, then went to the station. He told Sergio that Maddy's real name might have been Margie.

"Very possible. No Madeline West came here, legally. She suddenly was here and building a house. She bought the land for next to nothing, back then. She has four hectares plus that cost her a thousand dollars, and they thought they had taken her for a bundle. That kind of land wasn't considered to be good for anything at all. The Taylors, who had homesteaded it for nine years, would have given it to her, almost. It was the old

ROP. She could have owned it by living on it for two years and filing.

"It could be this one. She came then. All you needed to go anywhere was a birth certificate. Marjorie Williams. They didn't even check the identification. Anyone who came to these islands were considered stupid and weird to start with.

"She disappeared at the same time Madeline West started building that place. She signed her name as West. No one questioned it or cared. She got her permanent residence in ... ninety three. All she had to show then was ownership of property and a regular income. She had the property and had money in the bank. Welcome to Panamá!

"Now, maybe I can find something about her. It would help to know where she was from."

Clint called Judi, who didn't know. She gave him Yveth's number. He called and asked her if she knew where Maddy was from.

"Maddy? Well, I remember once she said she was from Texas. We were talking about that famous song, El Paso, and she said she was from there. Another time she told Carolina she was from Tempe, Arizona. She told Armando she was from Denver, Colorado. That was when they had those avalanches and you could go to jail if you made a loud noise or something. He said she claimed to know people in jail there, but not for noise. She knew a lot about San Francisco. The one in California. She also knew a lot about Philadelphia. In Pennsylvania.

"Where she was really from, I don't care. I think she had a bad husband and wanted to never see him again or something. I know she had an aunt and uncle in Kentucky. She said he knew all about the big war, there was a world war then, you know. She said he talked about going to Mexico when the United States got involved.

"We played bridge, sometimes. I was never good at it, but she was.

"I suppose you're looking for who did that to her. I hope you catch them and do the same to them!"

"We certainly plan to try," Clint said. "Thanks. It helps a lot." He hung up before she started reminiscing again.

"You notice where she was supposedly from? Often where there are US mints?" Sergio asked.

"And dear Uncle Joe wanted to go to Mexico."

Sergio sighed and went back to the computer. Clint took another and started a search. Sergio would look for information about her. He would look for a loss of a half ton of gold.

Suddenly, Sergio said, "Clint? She first came to Panamá in forty two with her mother. They brought in a truckload of household goods that were stored in a warehouse owned by a friend. They went back to the states after less than a month."

"What happened in seventy seven that made her come here?"

"Hmmm. Father deceased forty two. Killed when an armored truck he was guarding was hijacked in Mexico City. It isn't known if he was shot by the hijackers or if it was friendly fire. He was in a crossfire.

"Mother deceased March seventy seven. Heart failure. A month before she moved here."

"We might have our connection!"

"Let's see what kind of theories we can come up with, now," Sergio suggested. "We've learned a chronological order. Maybe we can add little bits and pieces.

"She came from the states to Panamá with her mother while the war was on. They brought that safe and stored it there until her mother died. She came here immediately, built that house, and brought her things from the warehouse, including the safe, with her.

"It was easy to get the safe here during the war. All they looked for was weaponry, and not even much of that, here.

"Her father set up the original deal where they stole the armored truck with its cargo of a safe full of gold. You noticed that the report didn't say what was in the truck. We can assume it was put there by some little dictator or arms dealer or such who could better afford to lose the gold than to have it known he even held any such thing.

"I'd say the uncle set it up. I'd say the father wasn't killed by friendly fire the way it was meant in the report. If the uncle was there, he made damned sure the father didn't survive that encounter. Considering what's happened, I can assume the uncle was the wife's brother.

"What have I left out – except ninety percent of it?"

"We have to trace the uncle. If he's been in jail since ... no. He would be a hundred years old. There's something else. There's some reason this happened now.

"We know we have to trace that uncle and we know we'll have to learn all we can about that hijacking. There's something there. Maddy didn't get any social security from the states. Where did she get whatever she got? Who sent her money every month? Why?"

"Clint, was that mold you found ever used? Was it tarnished by heat or was there a little residue?"

"I considered that. No."

"Then why was it there? She wouldn't have any reason to hide an unused mold. It would be in the house or the bodega, where the tools are."

"So. We should have printed that mold."

"I did. Yours and mine. It was wiped. The person who put it there wore gloves."

"There was a bar missing from that safe. Maybe two. She was living on whatever it brought. She arranged, somehow ... what's the matter?"

Sergio was laughing. "What would you do if you

had some money and wanted a regular fixed income from it? Income that would be put into your account at specific times? A way you can get residence here by proving regular income?"

"A CD?"

"One that pays on the second Wednesday each month."

"Call the bank."

Sergio called. Juan said he was surprised he hadn't asked from the first. They weren't allowed to volunteer information at the bank. She had a CD for two hundred fifty thousand that paid her a thousand dollars per month, deposited directly into her account. The account had more than a hundred thousand in it. They were looking for an heir. She withdrew two hundred dollars every second Wednesday of each month.

"I think that would have ... how long has that CD been in there? How many times was it renewed?"

"What do you mean?" Sergio looked puzzled. He called the bank and asked Juan.

"It was deposited in nineteen eighty nine and is renewed each two years."

"It took her ten years to find the combination. She probably started at four zeroes and simply went one and zeroes, two and zeroes until she hit it. She could have tried three quarters of the possibilities in ten years," Clint said. "If she hadn't hit it then, she would have kept on until she did. She didn't have much to do, other than that.

"Now we have to trace her and her family. We can use this as a base. We know what happened. We need to put the names and dates into it and we may come up with a killer. We may even come up with a killer and that ninety percent of the story we haven't figured yet."

"I've put out an information request over the entire United States, with concentration in the mid-south and southwest," Sergio answered. "I'm concentrating on birth certificates. It's all too possible, considering the time, she didn't ever have a passport. So long as people stay out of trouble, we don't much care, here – or didn't.

"I also have checks on all foreigners who have visited this island in the past month and who are still here. Maybe we can add a name from her past to a name from today and get an answer. That happens at least one percent of the time."

"I'll go home and spend some time with Tyna and Nito. Maybe Judi found something."

"If anyone can, she can!"

Clint waved and went out to his moto to head for home. Judi was sitting talking with Tyna, Earl and Ben, two other neighbors. She didn't learn much he didn't know about Maddy, but she did find a couple of things that might be related.

"There's a man, about fifty five, I'd say, who inserted himself into the conversation at The Grill. We were talking about it and he was at the next table. He said he was from the same town as her. Madiston, Texas. He was interested because of that. He heard they found a safe full of jewels and gold.

"I asked him where heard that. I'm a friend of the investigator, who only said there was a safe that you didn't have the combination for. He said he heard it down by the water taxi. A big black man was talking about it.

"I decided to scare him a bit. I said that was that CIA man. They call him 'Blackie.' He has a habit of making up things to see how people will react. Jim saw what I was doing. He said the ass was a rank amateur. He never stopped to see how much someone already knew before he dropped a bait line. When *he* worked in the agency, they were trained a hell of a lot better than today's lot.

"Reynolds! That was his name! He didn't hang around, after that."

Clint said that might help. He called Sergio. "See how many people are named Reynolds who are here as tourists or whatever. Also, try to find something about her from Madiston, Texas."

Sergio had never heard of any Madiston, Texas. Neither had Clint. He would check. "I'm running into a lot of brick walls. There are a lot of people with hidden pasts in this one!"

Clint walked around the town for awhile, but didn't run into Reynolds. He went to the police station to discuss how they could get the gold and safe out of there without the whole world finding out about it. Clint saw Basilio in his boat by the water taxi dock and called him to the police dock. He asked how they could manage it. Sergio shook his head..

"Well, I can get my sons to help. We can take the gold from the house with Nando's horse to my boat and can take it to your house. You can move the safe, then. We will then take it to the police station, right here. We can put a little gold in a big box that would be the right weight for books. Fifty or sixty libros in a box. I can carry ten boxes for one time. Four trips. I will charge six dollars for one trip, ten dollars for the horse, and twenty dollars for Nando and his brother. It will take three hours."

"Okay," Clint answered, while Sergio stared in disbelief. "When can we do it?"

"I have four people for Red Frog. One hour. I go get them at six, so there is plenty of time. I will need twenty dollars to start. I need fuel for the boat."

Clint gave him thirty dollars. He nodded and got

in his boat to pick up the people waiting on the water taxi dock.

"We'd better get some boxes. There's a good supply outside the China," Clint said.

"I don't believe you! You just contracted for thirty million dollars in gold to be secretly moved for fifty dollars!"

"Basilio's a friend. He's a Ngobe. What's difficult about that?"

Sergio shook his head. He and Clint went to the market, where the cardboard boxes were thrown into a cage outside. They selected several about the same size and headed back to the station. They threw them in back of the truck and got in. Emilio asked if he should drive. Clint said they were going to pack up a lot of things at Maddy's place to bring them for storage in the department. It would waste too much of the people's money with a driver. Sergio said he would be in charge until they returned. They didn't expect anything, but call him if they needed the truck or anything.

They went to the house. Clint stopped on the way. They picked up several more cardboard boxes and all the Styroform forms there, which was a lot. The places sold electronics that came with thick formed Styrofoam shock absorbing packaging.

Clint opened the safe. They took ten of the bars

out. He packed the boxes with the bars among Styrofoam pieces and made a layer of books on top. He sealed the boxes with duct tape.

Basilio's son came with a horse and they put four of the boxes in the net slings. He took them to the boat and came back for another load. Clint put eight boxes in the truck for Sergio to take back to the station.

"The evidence room won't hold all this," Sergio warned, nervously.

"It doesn't go in the evidence room. Back to the side where they knocked down that separator wall behind the old holding cell. Stack the boxes *carelessly* back there. I'll come with Basilio long before you get all these inside and put on an act that will guarantee nobody will dare bother them."

Sergio shrugged and looked exasperated, got in the truck, and drove off. Clint went with the load of boxes and got in the boat with Basilio while the sons brought the rest of the boxes to the little dock the Indios used. Nando sat on the boxes and smoked a cigarette while his brother went for more boxes from the house.

Clint and Basilio came to the dock, where Clint told the two officers there to grab some boxes and help unload them. He took a box in and to the place where Sergio and another officer were stacking the boxes. When they were all in the area

Clint asked Sergio which were mysteries and which were historic. They hadn't marked them and he would have to check. He felt historic novels were more important, even though he was personally sure she didn't have anything in the books but books.

Sergio looked at him strangely and said he wasn't sure.

Clint tore the tape off of one they had stacked and opened it. He read the spines of the books there. "Shit! Mystery!" He tore another and said that was historical. Those would all be in the flatter boxes, because those were the ones they were using in that section. He put his box to one side and moved several of the flatter boxes to one stack. He tore open another and announced that should do it. The historical were all in the six flatter boxes.

He roughly tossed the other boxes in a careless stack as Basilio returned with another load. They brought them in and he went for another. By now, the officers were getting tired of it, but dared not say anything. After all, Sergio was their boss!

Basilio brought the last and Clint paid him. They stacked them and were leaving when Sergio started to put the padlock on the door.

"Don't lock it yet. I'll want to go over a few of them later. I'll lock it when I leave.

"Sergio, you have the truck and these three officers. Do you think you can bring that safe? We can put it back here until we get the expert from Panamá City to open it. I don't think there'll be much of anything in it. She obviously hadn't opened it in a long time."

"Okay. It *is* evidence, because she was killed because she wouldn't open it for someone. We can't treat it like it was books. As soon as it's in here, be sure the place is locked when you leave. We'll catch hell if it's not secured."

"Yeah, I guess. Okay."

Sergio and the officers left. Clint went across the street to the little café for some late lunch and sat around trading gossip, then sighed and went back to the "books" when the safe was brought in. He helped them unload the heavy safe onto a dolly cart to take it back to the book stacks. They put it against the wall, face to the wall. Sergio said to turn it around.

"Why?" Clint asked.

"Because we can't open it that way."

"We can't, anyhow!"

"But the expert from Panamá City can."

"Oh, yeah. I forgot he was coming. I ... Sergio, did you keep that notebook page from the shelf? The one under the dictionary?"

Sergio looked a question. Clint showed him a

slip of paper hanging out of his pocket where the other officers couldn't see.

"You put it in your pocket."

"Oh." Clint reached in his front pockets and brought out the slip.

"I think this will be the combination. I can't see what else it could be. It's a series of four phone numbers. The combination's there."

Now Sergio did look confused. He shrugged.

Clint went to the safe door and tried several combinations of numbers. On the sixth, the handle turned.

"I knew she would have it somewhere in code! Didn't I *say* she would?" He said, smugly. He swung the door open. There was nothing in the safe. Nothing at all.

"Well, *that* sure as hell didn't solve our case for us! Shit!" Sergio cried.

"Damn it to fucking *hell!*" Clint cried. "We were so *sure* there would be something here!"

They went out cursing. "Lock the fucking door!" Sergio demanded.

"Why? There isn't anything in there!"

"Don't give me any of your shit! Lock it the fuck, anyhow!" Sergio seldom said anything past "Maldición!"

They went into Sergio's office and slammed the door. The other officers went timidly to the front.

They had never seen Sergio so bravo.

"I think we pulled that off perfectly!" Sergio said. "I see why you packed the books on top and why you looked in the boxes. Panameños are *not* going to be interested in books, especially books written in English."

"And we're so disappointed that our answers we were so smug about finding weren't in that safe you've gone into almost a rage. The ever level-headed Sergio Sanchez, totally pissed!

"Now we can transfer the gold back into the safe, somehow, when no one's around."

"No. It stays right there. We'd have to explain why we suddenly had four boxes of books where we had forty."

Clint nodded.

"Clint, there's a little of the things we requested from the states here. The Reynolds information is here. Madiston, Texas, is coming in right now."

"We can hope there's something in it. I think we can, have already, figure what happened, in a broader sense. A truckload of gold was hijacked, one of the hijack gang was eliminated at that time. He had a daughter and wife who, through the brother of the wife, ended up with the gold the wife brought to Panamá during the war. The daughter moved to this island when no one wanted anything to do with the islands and built a house. She moved the gold to the house and spent years finding the combination to a safe. She purchased a CD with one bar of that gold and has lived off the interest for years. Someone from the past found where she was hiding, probably after spending a lot of time in jail – and that part I don't quite accept – and came here to claim the gold, or a part of it. She wouldn't cooperate, he killed her."

"I agree to the point that she cashed in a bar and bought a CD to collect interest she's lived off for some years. We're out of information to base anything on, at that point. Maybe something here will clear up more of it. All I'm interested in is who killed her."

Sergio nodded and picked up a data sheet. "Reynolds, Franklin John. Sixty two years. Born Madiston, Texas. Lived in Houston. Ran a small pawn shop specializing in jewelry and precious metals. Moderately successful. Tourist. Came to this country eighteen days ago. Staying at the Sagitario.

"Not much. Here's Madiston. His father was Eugene John Harold Reynolds, mother Esther Janette Williams – and Maddy's real name was Williams. An Aunt?"

"Much too possible."

"Hmm. Father deceased, heart failure, Folsom Prison, June seven, ninety six. Armed robbery and assault with firearm, automatic life because commission of felony murder during hijack of armored vehicle, Houston, Texas.

"Mother resident Marmont, Arkansas, ninety six through April, this year. Deceased April four, this year. Age eighty eight. Natural.

"The mother's income was unknown. She had a CD ... the other gold bar? Before Maddy found the combination? I don't get that!"

"No. Probably it was something from another

hijacking or robbery. They never opened the safe.”

“Eugene John Harold Reynolds is going to be the uncle of Marjorie Williams, isn’t he?”

“‘Have been,’ but I think so.”

“So! Son of the uncle knows about the gold and finds where Maddy is when Mama buys it. He comes down here to get his share of the gold. He doesn’t get anything past pissed off enough to kill her.”

“It doesn’t quite fit, but there is a connection, I think.”

“Well, he’s here and she’s dead. He has some hard explaining to do!”

“Not until you can prove his father and mother were who we’re thinking they were. We have to get the history of Maddy-Marjorie to be able to connect them. With what we have, any half-assed lawyer can argue that we haven’t shown that Reynolds is any relation whatever of Maddy.”

“That information is here. Let’s see.” Sergio read several sheets of data. “Marjorie Williams was born in Madiston, but she wasn’t Williams’ daughter. She was adopted at birth. Her natural parents’ names are legally sealed by agreement of all parties.

“I had a check of the name, Madeline West, made in Madiston. There was nothing.”

"Can you get in touch ... no! Who else was part of that hijack? Maybe we can tie Reynolds into it that way."

Sergio called the computer girl in an asked her to find what she could about a hijack in Mexico on that date. She would have any information she could find in an hour. Clint and Sergio went to Clint's for a delicious dinner. Judi came by to say that Reynolds was staying at the Sagitario and had started asking questions about who traded in gold in Bocas Town the day he arrived. He was told to try three places in Changuinola for gold worth more than a hundred dollars or so. He had then gone to Changuinola and had returned, asking about Maddy, and did she have a safe deposit box or anything. He was told she had a big safe.

"So. He probably didn't kill her. He connected a lot of gold and that safe in the minds of the local hoods," Sergio suggested.

"Maybe," Clint replied. "That's one of several strong possibilities, a couple of which have local hoods involved."

Sergio nodded. It seemed more logical that a hired hood would get mad enough to kill anyone before they had what they came after.

"We have to know a lot more about Maddy," Clint said, tiredly. "This all seems surreal. Ghosts from the past, gold bullion, and the cavalry coming in to save the day, but don't.

"We have all of it except the thing I'm after, I suppose. I couldn't care less about the gold or the hijacking or whatever except where it connects to who killed Madeline West."

They talked awhile, then went back to the station. There was a data sheet on Sergio's desk. It was from Mexico City.

"Okay," Sergio said. "The hijacking was listed as a truck carrying items owned by a client of the bank, ID remains uncertain, but suspected of being a person from ... Germany?

"The client stated that motive for the hijacking was unknown. There was, supposedly, little of real value to anyone in the safe. There was a question asked at the time because of the manifest. It reads ... there's a copy ... one security vault, sixty cubic feet, two thousand one hundred pounds. Contents unknown. Insured for fifty thousand dollars, US.

"Clint, that volume and weight could only have been gold! Silver would have been two hundred or more pounds less!

"Perpetrators unknown. Wanted for murder during a robbery. Guard/driver killed. Policeman injured. Suspected to be Unknown Williams, Unknown West, Unknown Reynolds: informant.

"Well, we can connect Williams and Reynolds

with this, but not the one alive now."

"Sergio, get any information you can on West from Madiston."

"Yes. It seems quite the coincidence that she would use the name of Madaline West when her father was implicated in a hijack with a West."

He called the computer girl and asked that she got data about anyone named West in Madiston, Texas, in nineteen thirty five through forty. They waited. She'd already established an information link with them. This would be a matter of the old records that had later been put on the computer. Madiston was a small town that was smaller in the thirties. What they called a "One horse town" then. She brought in a sheet twenty minutes later to hand to Sergio.

"Okay! Two Wests in Madiston area then. Lawrence Hastings West, husband of Marjorie Fields-West. Had farm near town. He was an accountant and had a little hobby shop where he and his wife designed and produced silver and turquoise jewelry. Filed for bankruptcy in thirty nine.

"Frances Jean West, spinster sister of Lawrence.

"Medical. I figured we'd want that part. Little record, Lawrence. One time for broken arm. Wife was treated regularly for five months for gastrointestinal problems, nineteen thirty nine.

The records are sealed as to what the problem was.

"Okay! Marjorie had a baby in thirty nine, they were destitute, their good friends, the Williams, took the baby to raise. They stayed in contact. Papa and Williams made a deal where they would get a lot of money. How?"

"He worked with silver and went broke because silver became critical at that time because of the trouble starting in Europe. He knew about the connections with Mexico and the bank's vaults, where a lot of gold and silver was stored. People were beginning to hide their solid assets. A lot of people were taking their gold and silver out of the bank because there would be tracing if things got worse. They were damned well going to get worse and everyone knew it.

"West and Williams made a deal. They got Reynolds in on it. The accountant knew how to find when a German was going to move a lot of gold or silver, if he didn't know how much. There were going to be several large movements. The Trio went to Mexico City. Williams got a job as a guard for the bank's armored truck. They were going to move a safe that could only contain gold. The hijacking was arranged. Williams bought it because he would have gotten a split and because only he could connect them to it.

"The safe was stolen, but it was a big solid job that their safecracker couldn't get into. He didn't have the knowledge or equipment for anything that big. They didn't know what to do with it! The one person who could have solved that type problem was dead!

"His wife was alive. She could be convinced that he died because of the police, not them. He would have made a plan that she knew about. She could be convinced to handle it.

"It worked, in a major way. She used what was probably his plan to move the safe to Panamá for storage until they could open it.

"Now, the conjecture gets 'way out.

"She knew damned well who was responsible for hubby's getting knocked off. She decided to smack them in the puss with it. She would move the safe the way hubby had planned, then would do her own thing about it. She probably didn't give a hot damn about the gold, but she was going to see they never got an ounce.

"She goes back to the states. Maybe there was an anonymous tip about Reynolds' doings. He ended up in the pen for life. West was told that made it too hot for them. Sit on the gold for a year or two until it had died down. He was no problem. Here was this meek accountant whose daughter she was raising. He was mortally terrified he would be exposed. She sympathized and said they should just forget about the gold. She would arrange it so his daughter got it. They didn't need it. It was too risky, but the daughter was just eleven years old. She couldn't be charged with anything, in the future. She didn't have a clue as to what they had done.

"Her plan worked perfectly. She lived fairly well until she died. The daughter knew the whole thing and decided she would actually have that gold, someday.

"That plan worked as well. She was sitting on millions in gold and living on what she needed. That gold sitting there was something to consider as her revenge on the lot of them for killing her stepfather. Her real father had abandoned her. He didn't deserve a nickle.

"Then Reynolds original died in prison. He left something for sonny boy that told him who to look for and where to look. In all those years in prison, there was sure to be someone who had come across Marjorie, somewhere! The Wild Bill thing probably clinched it. Someone would have definitely said they had been in Bocas and knew Wild Bill or someone who knew him. A few questions and Maddy was mentioned as the type he preyed on, but she didn't have anything, so was safe.

"Sonny boy comes and starts asking questions. He finds Maddy and wants a deal.

"Sergio, that mold was brought here by him. He probably said all they had to do was melt it down and remold it without the stamp and no one could ever prove where it came from. I think he went there with that mold after hiring some local goons to scare her to where she'd be willing to deal. The hoods had put two and two together and had come up with four. They were going to get a lot of gold – but she wouldn't cooperate. She knew them. She could identify them. She died. He went out there and found her, hid the mold, and came back into town to act like the innocent.

"Far enough out for you?"

"Probably close to the truth, in most parts. You have to find who did the job and make them give us Reynolds. I don't think you can."

"I think I can."

"So. You think you can find who killed Maddy? How?" Sergio asked.

"I have to make a few local hoods think I know more than I do," Clint replied.

"Can you?"

"I can give it the old college try."

"I wish you luck. You'll need it!"

They chatted awhile. It was late. This would wait until tomorrow. He went home to be with his wife and child. They went to the Lemon Grass for Thai food. Clint carried Nito most of the time. They were raising Nito in the Indio tradition. He was always in contact with one parent or another. He felt secure. He didn't cry or act up, a sharp contrast to the black family with a little girl close to the same age who kept crying and screaming in what had to be a temper fit until they were asked to leave. Nito looked at Clint like he was asking, "What the hell is wrong with that brat?"

"She's being raised to act like that."

"What?" Tyna asked.

"Nito can't figure why anyone would act like that. I told him."

"Oh." She didn't question that an eight month old child could communicate that thoroughly.

They went home about ten. Dave, their weird musician/ botanist/writer friend, came in with a new face, a semi-pretty gringo with a guitar of her own. They had played a few numbers. He introduced her as Emily. It was an altogether pleasant night.

In the morning, Clint went to The Golden Grill to have coffee and to chat with the regulars. Reynolds came in and sat with them. He went to the counter to order and Jim said he wasn't invited to join them, he just did. When he came back Jim said, "Oh. Clint. John, wasn't it?"

"F. John Reynolds. Pleased to meet you.

"You're the detective who works for the police here?"

"I work with them on some murder cases," Clint replied. "It's sort of a specialty."

"Ah! You're working on that West woman's case?"

"Yes. A bit. Her stepfather and your father were business partners before your father went to the pen for life, I think."

He spilled his coffee all over himself. "*Yeep*! How did you ...? What...?"

"It's all public record. She wasn't from here, though she'd been here for some years. You told people you were from the same town, she was murdered while you were here. You'd have to know you'd be investigated."

"I did *not* kill anyone!"

"Oh, we know. That would have to prove not to be of benefit to you. She had a couple of hundred thousand in the bank, but you aren't a relative and there was no will naming you. No motive. No profit."

"I hear there was a safe in her house that you couldn't open. It's supposed to be full of money."

"We opened it. She had the combination right there in a book. There's nothing in it."

"Nothing?"

"Nothing. Not even dust. It's at the station. I can arrange that you look in it, if you want, but don't see why."

"But she had money in the bank?"

"What we found, yes. It seemed she was one for using aliases, so she could have fifty million in an offshore bank under a corporate name and we'd never know it until a hundred years have passed and there isn't any action in the account. By then, it'd be more than a hundred fifty million. Happens sometimes."

He looked like he would cry.

"Well, I mean, why would anyone kill anyone like that. There had to be a reason."

"Some of the local hoods knew about the safe. Everybody does. They heard you asking about gold. They added it up. They tried to force the combination out of her. I don't know why she wouldn't give it, unless she could identify them and knew they would have to kill her if she gave it to them. They killed her anyway. We'll find them. We always do."

"How? I mean, if they didn't get anything?"

"They left something there. Everyone does. Anywhere you go, you leave a trace in DNA. They're big on DNA here."

Jim was staring at him and caught on. "Yes. That Nambo character. He thought he would never be caught when he killed Feeny. He used gloves and a disguise and covered his face and everything else. He sneezed or something. He thought he was away and Scot free when they picked him up ten days later. His DNA was the only one there that wasn't supposed to be there.

"If you do anything illegal here, wait a few days until the labs process all the DNA from the scene. If you had no reason to be there, you're prison bound."

"They'd have to prove you did ... whatever, not only that your DNA was there!"

"Nope! You're guilty until proven innocent, here," Clint replied. "It saves a hell of a lot more innocent people than the other way. They have the strong evidence of guilt before they make an arrest. Very few get away with much. The proof that you leave DNA everywhere is proven a few million times."

"It is?"

"Sure! What do you think a bloodhound uses to identify the right one, every time?" Jim asked. "The days of stupid technicalities and that kind of thing are almost over. Here."

Reynolds looked like he would faint. Clint winked at Jim, who pointed to him and raised his eyebrows. Clint nodded yes and shook his head no. Jim would know he was fishing.

"What was that for?" Reynolds asked.

"What?"

"Nodding and shaking your head."

"Sore neck. I don't realize I'm doing it."

He looked suspicious, but didn't say more. He soon finished his coffee and left, saying he had to check to see if his funds were deposited at the bank.

"He didn't do it," Jim said. "What?"

"No, he didn't do it, *personally*," Clint corrected. "That's why I mentioned that we would catch the local hoods who did it."

Jim nodded. "So. Now what?"

"We see who he goes straight to."

Jim nodded again. Clint paid his tab and left. If Reynolds was going to the bank, he was certainly taking a round-about path! He had walked off to the left. The bank was to his right. To his left was toward the less amiable part of town.

Clint stayed two blocks behind. Reynolds went to the Grand Kahuna and turned right. Clint turned down the block before. If Reynolds was watching to see if he was being followed, he would be around the corner, waiting for the follower.

Clint waited. Three minutes later, Reynolds passed and went on to sixth street, then to the big China and back along the scraped road. He went to a house and called, "Buenos!" a couple of times. A big fat woman came to ask what he wanted.

"Striker or Fast Freddy."

"Not here. Almirante." She went back inside.

So. Striker and Fast Freddy. He knew how to find his killers. It would now become a matter of connecting them to Reynolds. Clint went home. Fast Freddy had a fast boat, thus the nickname. Clint would have it noted when they got back to Bocas Town. He went home.

Judi came over after a little while and said she might have something Clint would like to know. "Fast Freddy and Striker are in Changuinola right now, spending a lot on fancy clothes.”

“Thanks, Judi. That ties most of it up.” He called Sergio. They would keep the two and Reynolds under surveillance.

“Want to go fishing?” Clint asked Judi and Tyna.

“Sure! I guess that really did tie it up!” Judi said. “I’ll go get my stuff. Pan or big?”

“Which do you want?”

“Tuna are running. I want to catch one more than a hundred twenty four pounds. I have a contest with Ben and Earl.”

“I’ll pick you up in fifteen minutes.”

Tyna and Nito were prepared and in the boat, Judi was waiting on her deck. Clint picked her up and they headed outward between Carenero and Bastimentos, then turned south and toward Crawl Cay. There were several boats out. Clint scanned the horizon and turned more northward and outward. He went out about three kilometers and headed south again. Tyna and Judi both saw what he’d seen and rigged their tackle. Clint took Nito and steered toward the gulls flying and diving a short way away. He slowed to about five KPH and went along in front of the moving flight. Judi hooked one as Tyna got a strong strike that didn’t hook. Clint kept the boat at a good angle as Judi brought the fish alongside. It would weigh about eighty pounds. They released it and went back through. Both Tyna and Judi hooked fish at the same time. When the tuna are schooling, they are feeding. They'll hit anything that comes through. Tyna's was about sixty pounds, perfect for their freezer, so they kept it. Judi's was about forty pounds and they released it.

Ten minutes later Tyna hooked a big one that broke the two hundred pound test line. Less than a minute later Judi hooked a big one and fought it for more than twenty minutes. They brought it alongside. It would be well over a hundred fifty pounds. They struggled it aboard and weighed it, 186 pounds, took some pictures, and shoved it back into the water. It laid for a minute, then turned and dove.

Judi took the wheel, Tyna took Nito, and Clint fished. He caught one that would weigh about a hundred pounds, then another that would go fifty or so. It had been a very good afternoon. They returned to Clint's house about four thirty. Clint called Sergio, who said Freddy and Striker were back. Nothing else new.

The trio met Ben and Earl and went into town to El Ultimo Refugio for a delicious dinner. As they were leaving they saw Striker going into the VIP. Ben and Earl and Judi and Gino, a friend of Judi's, were going over to the Pickled Parrot. Clint, Tyna, and Nito went home for the night.

In the morning, Clint spent some time doing the things he'd meant to do when this started. He saw that an orchid he'd crossed had a capsule ready to flask, so he called Dave, who had a system for growing the seeds. He came over and took the capsule. They talked a bit, then Dave left. Sergio called to say that Reynolds might be leaving on the eight o'clock flight in two days. Clint said to not let on that they knew anything yet. Sergio said he wanted to make some kind of arrangement to get that gold out of there. It made him nervous. Clint said to set something up where they could take the gold bullion to Panamá City or something. Maybe they could load it back into the safe and put the safe on the ferry with a guard or whatever would work. Sergio said he thought it would be a good idea to load the safe and the books into a small cargo container and into a truck that would take it. The police could arrange for the truck to look like a standard carrier.

"Whatever. I don't care about gold." He would leave it to Sergio.

"Aren't you afraid I'd run off with it?"

"No. Anyone else, yes. You, no. Besides, what would you do with it? Hide it in a house somewhere for thirty years?"

That got him the one finger salute.

He went to The Golden Grill to talk with the

regulars. One, Tom, didn't put in his two cents worth, for once. Clint didn't like the phony gossip and had come awfully close to smacking him a few times when The World's Greatest Expert on Everything was running his mouth about something he knew nothing about.

Reynolds came to join them after about an hour. He and Tom seemed to hit it off (It figured!). They chatted like none of the others were there. Finally, Reynolds said, "Did the DNA thing find anything?"

"They have three to identify, so they'll be locals. The rest were all residents or locals who volunteered because they'd been regular visitors and such. They have to get racial markers to know who to take samples from," Clint answered.

"Supposing they won't allow samples?"

"Not allow? Oh. This isn't the states. You don't have to allow anything."

"What do you mean, racial markers?"

"Each race has a basic framework that the individual markers overlay in specific patterns," Tom said, authoritatively. "There is a definite pattern that comes through, even on mixed races, particularly blacks and orientals. They can trace back to an individual tribe, in many cases, or even to a specific ancestor."

Reynolds was looking nervous and a bit scared,

now. Fast Freddy and Striker were blacks. He was Anglo-Saxon.

"I think Sergio said there was a basic black matrix for two of them. Maddy didn't get along with the blacks. That leaves us with one hell of a question. Why was that DNA in her house?

"The other didn't seem to him to have the black matrix overlay. Underlay."

"Maybe a maid?"

"Maybe a maid what?" Jim asked. "Oh. Maddy didn't use a maid. She took care of her house by herself. She was spry for her age. She didn't like blacks, so wouldn't have a black maid. She did get along with the Indios. That has a definite matrix that's got a lot in common with certain oriental sub-races."

They chatted for a bit. It seemed that Tom had studied something about DNA on the net and did know something about the science. Wonders never cease!

"Whatever, they'll get it down to the individual pretty fast, now. They don't have a lot to check," Jim said. "Clint, I hear Judi has the upper hand in her contest with Ben and Earl about the biggest tuna?"

"She caught a hundred eighty five pounder. Gives them something to shoot for."

"Judi? The Japanese woman? Goodlooking?"

Reynolds asked. "I saw her with someone they called Ben in the Toro Loco. Ben and some other guy were with her. The two guys look like Mr. Universes or something, but the way they always had an arm around each other makes you wonder how Mr. they are."

"Ben and Earl? They're married, if not by the church. The way most are married here."

"Oh. Maybe I was mistaken. I thought they were a little close. If they're married, I guess not."

"No. *They* are married," Jim said. "That's not considered so unusual, here. Nobody cares who anybody else sleeps with."

Reynolds was staring in shock. "They're gay?!"

"Didn't you just say you thought they might be? Why be shocked when you find you were right?" Jim asked.

"But ... but, just like that?"

"They aren't hiding anything from anybody," Clint answered. "Jim, did that party, the wake, come off as good as it did last year? I was in Tula, so couldn't make it."

They chatted a bit more, then Clint went home to check his e-mail and such. There wasn't much new there, either. He and Tyna spent the evening watching a Will Smith movie on TV. It was fun. They cuddled and played like a couple of horny teenagers.

It was just after six the next morning when Clint got a call from Sergio.

"Clint? Striker was shot and killed last night, just after midnight. Fast Freddy has disappeared. His boat's gone."

"Where is Reynolds?"

"So far as I know, in the Sagitario."

Clint dressed quickly and headed for the station. Something was a long way from making sense. If Reynolds was in the hotel, who killed Striker?

There were probably several people who had good reason, but the timing said that it had to be Reynolds. What had happened with Fast Freddy?

Sergio had an order out to find Fast Freddy and take him into protective custody.

"Let's go talk to Reynolds," Clint suggested. "We have to find out how he did it."

Sergio nodded and looked grim.

They went to the hotel and Sergio called a man across the street working on welding together a fancy gate to ask about Reynolds. He took out a pad and said he took over from Santo at eight. Reynolds was on the porch with the redheaded woman from Ireland. He went inside at nine thirty and didn't come back out. He didn't leave the hotel. A lot of people came and went. He had their codes and times. The redheaded woman left at a quarter to ten and returned at eleven forty two. She was the only one observed being with Reynolds at any time.

They went inside and asked about Reynolds' room. Number twenty eight. In back, just past the stairs.

Clint asked about the redheaded woman. Her name was Shannon O'Shaunesy. 29, right across from Reynolds.

They went up and knocked on Reynolds' door. He answered in his pajamas and asked what they wanted. Clint said they had come to ask him some questions about Maddy West. His DNA was found in trace amounts in her house.

"Er, I was there for no more than five minutes. I went there because she was from my own home town. She made it very plain that she didn't care to know anyone from her past, particularly not from Madiston. I was told to stay away from her. I did. It was what made me curious when I heard she'd been killed."

"You should have come forth from the first," Sergio said, sternly. "It is a curious circumstance that you didn't."

"I didn't know anything! I didn't want to get involved!"

"The good old American way!" Clint said. "Work so hard not to become involved in any bad situation and instead become suspected. You should have told me at The Golden Grill."

"I really thought about that. I know it was a

mistake, but I didn't have anything to do ... I most certainly didn't kill her!"

"It wouldn't mean so much if another one whose DNA was found at her house hadn't been murdered last night," Sergio said. "That shines and entirely different light on it."

"But I was *here* last night!"

"You don't even want to know what time he was killed? Or where? Or how?" Clint asked.

"I was *here* all night!"

"I see. Were you with anyone? A lady? Anyone who can say you didn't leave the hotel?"

"I was with Shannon, if it was early. We talked on the porch until ten or so. I don't know exactly. We went to bed about then, I think. She's in the room across the hall."

Sergio went to knock on the door. It was the third round of knocks before she answered. She said she couldn't believe she slept so late.

Shannon was a stocky woman and had grey hair.

"Well, when you stay out later than you're used to you will tend to oversleep the next morning," Sergio said. "You were with Mr. Reynolds last evening? Until about ten o'clock?"

"Yes. Nine thirty or ten. I was tired and took a sleeping pill and went to bed. I believe he went to bed about the same time. He said he was going to."

Clint smirked. "But the taxi driver said he tried to pick you up over near sixth street, much later than that!" Clint cried. "You're the only one here with that red hair!"

"But I was here! I was asleep until you woke me up just now! I don't even know where sixth street is!"

"Then it was someone wearing your wig. Someone who knew you wouldn't wake up and give him away. Someone who tricked you into a position where you'd be suspected, not him."

Reynolds bolted for the stairs.

"Where in holy *hell* does he think he's going?" Sergio exclaimed. "This is an *island*!" He shook his head.

"And wearing pajamas?" Clint added. That got him a finger.

They were going down the stairs when Reynolds came back to say, "Okay. That was stupid. I panicked.

"Can I put on some decent clothes? I won't try to run again."

"Okay. Wouldn't do you any good. You can't get off the island.

"What happened to Fast Freddy?"

"I saw him first, down by the dock. I tricked him into running by telling him they found his DNA at Maddy's house. You were going to arrest him. He had to get out! Fast!

"I knew I couldn't handle both of them. He grabbed a bag he already had packed and left. I went to find Striker and shot him. The pistol's in the mangroves just before the Indian village.

"I would have gotten away with it if it wasn't for that taxi."

"There wasn't any taxi. Trickery works both ways," Clint said. "I could count on at least one taxi trying to pick you up that time of night back there."

"Damn! All I had to do was keep my big mouth shut!"

"It would have bought you one day, at the most, but you wouldn't be facing the second murder charge," Sergio said. "Get some clothes. You'll need a toothbrush and that kind of thing. We can get some breakfast on the way. I haven't had anything today."

"Just like that? No handcuffs or shackles?"

"Why? It's a damned island! You can't go anywhere, so why not be civilized?" Sergio said.

"How refreshing! A minute. You can come with me if you like."

"We'll wait here on the porch."

They waited a few minutes until Reynolds came out, carrying a backpack. He slipped it on and said he was as ready as he would ever be. They went to

Chitres and had a good breakfast, chatting about Southern Texas, then to the station.

"I just wish I knew what happened to all the the gold," Reynolds said.

"It's on its way to Panamá City, at the moment," Sergio answered.

"How much was there? Like Dad said? About five million dollars worth?"

"About twice that, back then. Thirty million now," Clint answered.

"Damn! And all I wanted was a lousy fifty grand to start a business!"

"Your luck sucks," Clint said.

As so many had said to Clint before, "You sort of go for understatement, don't you?"

"So. Now we have most of it," Sergio said, leaning back and toasting Tyna with his beer. "We had it figured a lot closer than I would believe. The gang who couldn't shoot straight or something. Keystone Kops.

"They picked up Fast Freddy in Changuinola, trying to get to Costa Rica. He gave us Reynolds all the way, mostly because he killed Striker. Reynolds laid out what he knew. It was very much like you thought.

"Well, guess we'll have to rustle up another murder for you! You get bored with nothing to do!"

"I'll pass."

C. D. Moulton's works are available on most major outlets as printed or e-books. CD writes the CD Grimes, PI, mysteries, the Det. Lt. Nick Storie mysteries, the Clint Faraday mysteries, the Flight of the Maita science fiction series, books on orchid culture and many others of many types. Mystery, adventure, intrigue, science fiction, humor, fantasy, paranormal, mild erotica, and factual.